A Dog
for Jesse

A Dog for Jesse

created by
Sharon M. Hart

written by
Emma Davis

illustrated by
Sandy Rabinowitz

A
LITTLE APPLE
PAPERBACK

A Parachute Press Book

SCHOLASTIC INC.
New York Toronto London Auckland Sydney

ISBN 0-590-41503-4

Copyright © 1989 by Parachute Press. All rights reserved. Published by Scholastic Inc. APPLE PAPERBACKS is a registered trademark of Scholastic Inc.

12 11 10 9 8 7 6 5 4 3 2 1   9/8 0 1 2 3 4/9

Printed in the U.S.A.   11
First Scholastic printing, February 1989

For Maggie and her friend Jesse

Contents

Chapter One

Jesse and Ginger

Jesse's eyes popped open. He sat up straight and gently put his hand on the dog sitting beside his bed.

"Ginger!" he said. "Stay!"

The setter had heard the noise too, and was wide awake. Her muscles twitched as she stared at the open doorway. Before Jesse could stop her, she leaped into the hall and began to bark.

"Sssh!" someone said.

Ginger obediently stopped. Jesse heard voices at the top of the stairs.

"Tim?" Jesse called. "Arden?" Where were his brother and sister going so early? he wondered. And why were they leaving without him?

Just then, Tim's lanky body appeared in Jesse's doorway. Arden was right behind him.

"Hey, Jess," Tim said. "You're up early."

"You're up early, too," Jesse answered. "Where are you going?"

Arden took a rubber band from her jeans' pocket and pulled her long, brown hair into a ponytail. "I'm meeting Joey at the stable," she said. "We're giving Glory an early-morning workout."

Jesse liked Joey. The trainer was wonderful with horses — and pretty good with kids, too.

Tim was already halfway down the stairs.

"Where are *you* going?" Jesse asked him.

Tim looked up from the landing. "I'm going to feed Frisky."

Frisky was a mink Gran had saved the same week she'd taken Ginger in. He and the dog were just two of the injured or abandoned creatures who made their home at River Oaks, the animal rescue farm. The farm also sheltered two elephants, a pair of llamas, one grizzly bear, a lioness, and about two hundred somewhat less exotic beasts. They thrived under Gran's skilled veterinary care, free to roam the 300-acre farm for the rest of their natural lives.

Jesse grabbed his robe off the bedpost, jumped out of bed, and followed his brother and sister downstairs.

"Need any help?" he asked.

"No thanks," Tim said.

Jesse stopped short on the bottom step, and Arden turned to look at him.

"Know what I wish?" Jesse said wistfully.

"What?"

At first Jesse didn't answer. He kept his eyes on his wiggling toes. "I wish Mom and Dad hadn't gone to Africa and left me here all alone," he finally said.

Arden looked surprised. "Jesse," she said, "I can't believe what you're saying. You know how hard it was for Mom and Dad to go. I'm sure they miss us at least as much as we miss them. You know we all agreed this trip was too good an opportunity for them to pass up. How often do wildlife photographers get the chance to spend a whole year on safari?

"Besides," she went on, "you're not exactly alone. What about Gran and Gramp, not to mention Tim and me? Don't *we* count?"

"Don't be mad," Jesse said. "Of course you count. But Gran and Gramp have each other. And so do you and Timmy. You're always going off on your own and leaving me behind."

"Oh, Jesse," Arden said. "Is that really what you think?"

"Yes," Jesse said accusingly. "Like right now. It isn't even eight o'clock, and you and Tim are all ready to go. I'll have to hang around here by myself all day."

"What about Ginger and Mortie?" Arden asked.

"Mortie!" Jesse cried. "He's just a dumb bird!"

Jesse felt ashamed talking this way. He really liked the mynah bird. But even though Mortie could talk, he wasn't much company.

"Okay, okay," Tim said. "Calm down. I admit you have a point. Listen," he told Jesse. "Frisky can wait a few minutes — he'll be okay. Right now I'm going to do something nice just for you."

"It's about time," Arden teased. "Isn't it, Jess?"

Jesse swallowed a smile. He was feeling better already.

"What?" he asked.

"I, Tim Quinn, am going to fix my Special Cheerer-Upper Mango Pancakes!"

Arden rolled her eyes. "Your pancakes *need* fixing," she said.

"Yeah," Jesse piped up. "This time, why don't you try using flour instead of cement mix?"

Tim clutched at his stomach as if he'd

5

been struck, then crumpled to the floor.

Arden started to laugh. But her eyes went wide when Tim didn't move. "Are you all right?" she said, bending over him anxiously.

"Gotcha!" Tim shouted. He flung out one hand and yanked Arden's ponytail. With the other, he mussed Jesse's curly red hair. Arden and Jesse squealed and wriggled away. Then they both began tickling him.

They were making so much noise, Gramp poked his head into the downstairs hallway. "Keep it down!" he barked. "I'm on the phone." Then he went back into his den, and closed the door behind him. Even so, Jesse, Tim, and Arden could hear his voice rising.

"I bet that's Gramp's lawyer," Jesse said. "He must be calling about the town houses again."

For the last several weeks a man named Sam Smith had been trying to buy off a big section of River Oaks. He wanted to clear the land and build a whole development of town houses.

Though Gramp kept insisting he wouldn't sell for any price, Smith kept calling the Quinns' lawyer with bigger and better offers for the land.

"I wish that guy would just give up," Arden said. "Why can't he understand that Gramp thinks animals have as much right to the land as people? Just think what would happen to them all if Gramp *did* sell! Where would they go?"

Arden's question was drowned out by Thomas Quinn's angry voice.

"Wow! Gramp is really upset now," Tim said.

They all heard their grandfather slam the phone down.

For a moment no one spoke. Then Tim's stomach rumbled loudly. Arden looked at Tim and Jesse. Jesse looked at Tim and Arden. Then all three began to giggle.

"I guess it's time for those pancakes," Tim said as they headed for the kitchen.

* * * *

Jesse was still eating when Arden scraped her last two pancakes into Ginger's dish. The setter gulped them down before Arden and Tim had even closed the kitchen door.

Jesse leaned down to pet Ginger, and she gave him a quirk slurp on the cheek. Then she lowered her head back down to her dish and licked it clean. Jesse

smiled at the sandpaper sound her tongue made.

You are so beautiful, he thought.

Ever since he could remember, Jesse had wanted a dog. It didn't matter to him that dogs weren't as wild or exotic as many of the animals at River Oaks. Dogs were what he loved best. And now — at last — he had Ginger.

Over and over he stroked her shiny, auburn coat. She had come to River Oaks with a bad cut, but had stayed on even after her wound had healed. "Ginger," he whispered. "Ginger." He hoped his grandparents would let Ginger stay at River Oaks forever.

Chapter Two

Gran to the Rescue

Gramp stomped into the kitchen and reached for the rest of the pancake batter. "Guess what *that* call was about," he said.

Jesse shifted in his seat. He knew Gramp didn't really expect an answer.

Gramp stood over the griddle and flipped the pancakes. "People need places to live, too," he said. "I know that. But there has to be a little more planning — a little more caring. Someone has to watch out for the wild animals."

Just then the kitchen door opened and Gran came in from her rounds. "What's all this serious talk so early in the morning?" Tansy Quinn said. "And on a

Sunday, no less." She put down her medical bag and turned to Gramp. "Sunday means a fat newspaper," she said. "Why don't you and Jesse drive into town and get one?"

As soon as he'd finished his pancakes, Gramp went upstairs for his wallet. While Jesse was waiting for him, the telephone rang and Gran answered it. Jesse could tell by her face that something was the matter.

"What's wrong?" he asked.

Gran put a finger to her lips. "Where did it happen?" she asked into the phone. "How badly is he hurt?"

Jesse sat glued to his chair. Who was the "he" Gran was talking about? Could it be his mother calling from Africa with bad news? Had something terrible happened to his father? Jesse held his breath.

Finally Gran hung up the phone and reached for her medical bag. She took one look at Jesse's face and smiled reassuringly. "Don't worry," she said. "The call wasn't about your dad."

Jesse's breath whooshed out in relief. He loved the way Gran seemed able to read his mind.

"There *is* an emergency, though," she added. "Tell Gramp I'll be bringing in a new patient."

"When?" Jesse asked.

Gran spoke in a rush. "In an hour or so," she said. And then she was out the door like a whirlwind.

Jesse got up and went tearing after her. "What *kind* of patient?" he cried. But Gran had already reached her jeep and was gunning the motor. She leaned out the window to answer him, but the roaring engine swallowed her words.

Disappointed, Jesse peered through the cloud of dust the jeep left behind. But his spirits lifted when he saw his grandfather heading toward the pickup truck.

"Gramp!" Jesse shouted. "Wait for me! I've got something important to tell you."

"Now hold on there, young man,"

Gramp said as Jesse began tugging at his sleeve.

Jesse quickly told Gramp about the emergency call and the new patient.

"What do you think Gran's bringing in?" Jesse asked. "Will you let me take care of it? How badly do you think it's hurt?" he blurted out before Gramp could answer his first question.

"I have no idea," Gramp said. "But she'd better get back soon. Otherwise you'll explode with curiosity and then she'll have *two* patients to worry about!"

Jesse tried to control himself. "I guess we'd better get going," he said in his most grown-up voice. "Come on, Ginger."

Ginger glanced at Jesse. Then she turned her attention to a squirrel that was scampering toward the office.

"Ginger, come *on!*" Jesse repeated in a louder voice.

Ginger gave the squirrel one last look before trotting over to Gramp's truck and jumping into the cab. Jesse flung an arm around her. You're my dog! he thought proudly.

Gramp drove out the entrance to the farm and onto the town road. As he passed the River Oaks Elementary School, he pointed at the tiny clapboard building. "Summer's almost over, Sport," he said. "Come September, this will be your school. How does it look to you?"

"Pretty good," Jesse answered. The school seemed just the right size. Best of all, there was a baseball field in back. And baseball was his favorite sport.

When they got to the general store, Gramp bought the last newspaper and surprised Jesse with a dozen fresh-baked sugar cookies to take back with them. Jesse immediately reached a hand inside the bag. "Mmm," he said. The cookies were still warm.

"Oh, no, you don't," Gramp said. "No head starts. Just let me take a peek at this paper here before we get going."

Jesse grinned at his grandfather. "Uh-uh. No head starts!" But when Gramp pulled out the Features section, Jesse peered over his arm.

All at once Jesse's eyes opened wide. "Wow!" he said. "Look at that!"

"This *is* a surprise," said Gramp. There on page one was a photograph of Jesse's parents and a long article about their exciting careers.

Jesse stood on tiptoe to get a better look. "There's even something about the farm," he said, following Gramp into the truck. They read every word of the article before heading back to River Oaks.

When they were almost home, Gramp noticed a boy walking along the side of the road. "I wonder who that fella is," he said. "I've never seen him before. He looks about Tim's age, but I can see he has something in common with *you*."

Jesse grinned as Gramp slowed the truck down. He knew exactly what his grandfather was talking about. On top of the boy's head was a New York Mets baseball cap. Jesse was a big Mets fan.

The boy turned in at the house just

down the road from the farm. "That's funny," Gramp said. "He's going into Mrs. Martin's house. She only moved here a couple of days ago, but I'm pretty sure she lives alone. I would have noticed if she had a son."

"Maybe he's her nephew or something," Jesse suggested.

As Jesse stared out the window, he caught the boy looking back at him. Somewhere he found the courage to wave. The boy didn't wave back, though. He didn't even smile.

Jesse turned away in embarrassment. But he didn't have time to worry about this unfriendly stranger, for just then he saw Gran driving toward the farm from the opposite direction.

"Gramp!" Jesse cried. "Let's go!"

Thomas Quinn floored the pedal in the pickup. Dust flew as he sped up the driveway and came to a stop beside Gran. Jesse leaped from the truck and put Ginger in the office. By the time he joined his grandparents at the jeep, Tim and Arden and Joey were already there.

Jesse looked inside the jeep. What had Gran brought? he wondered. An iguana? A rattler? There was no animal she would turn away.

Jesse peered closer, but whatever it was had burrowed under an old blanket. The blanket suddenly stirred, and Jesse's face lit up. A pair of big brown eyes were looking back at him, the dark swimming eyes of a dog. *Another dog!*

Chapter Three

The Problem With Pegleg

"There aren't many dogs that could survive an alligator attack," Gran said when she came out of her operating room an hour later. A few strands of hair had come loose from the knot she kept pinned on top of her head. Gran looked tired — but beautiful, Jesse thought.

"An alligator attack!" Tim gasped.

Tansy Quinn raised her eyebrows and nodded. "That's right," she said. "Fog was so thick this morning that the dog lost his way and fell into a pond. He was trying to scramble out when the 'gator got him."

A chill ran down Jesse's spine. He'd seen an alligator just a week ago. It had lifted its head through a carpet of water lettuce and looked right at him!

Arden's eyes widened. She reached for Jesse's hand and squeezed it. "What happened then?" she asked.

"Poor pup," Gran said. "The 'gator got part of his left hind leg."

"Oooh," Arden shivered.

"I know," Gran said. "It sounds awful, doesn't it? But don't worry. Our patient's doing fine. He'll be up and around in just a few days."

"So soon?" Tim said.

Gran nodded. "The most important thing is to make sure the wound doesn't become infected. And of course he'll have to get around on three legs — well, three and a half — from now on," she said sympathetically.

For a moment, Tim and Arden and Jesse said nothing. Then Arden asked, "What kind of dog is it?"

"That's kind of hard to say," Gran replied. "Mostly terrier, I'd guess — with maybe a little poodle thrown in."

"Does he belong to anyone?" Jesse wanted to know.

"Not exactly," Gran said. "He was with a young hiker who found him wandering along the road a week or so ago."

"What should we call the dog, Gran?" said Tim. "Does he have a name?"

Gran shook her head no.

"Let's call him Hobo," Arden suggested.

"He looks more like a Scruffy to me," Tim said.

An idea suddenly came to Jesse. "How about Pegleg?" he cried.

"Way to go," Tim, Arden, and Gran agreed.

The hiker visited the farm early the next day.

"I just wanted to see how my pal was doing," he told Jesse. "You know," he said, glancing fondly at Pegleg, "that little guy has a nose as good as a bloodhound's. He's always sniffing something out. Wait till you see all the gifts he brings you. He's better than Santa Claus!"

"Gifts?" Jesse said. "He brings you presents?"

The young man laughed. "Well, not exactly," he said. "Just stuff. Odds and ends. Things. You'll see."

"Will you be waiting around till Pegleg gets better?" Jesse wanted to know.

"No," the hiker said. "I wish I could, but I've got to get back home right away."

"What if Pegleg hadn't been hurt?" Jesse asked. "What if he could go with you right now? Would you take him?"

"I guess so," the hiker said. "He's not much to look at — not like your setter here — but I was really getting attached to him. He kind of grows on you. You'll see."

Jesse looked at Pegleg lying on the cushion Gran had given him and shrugged. At the same time he tightened his arm around Ginger.

★　★　★　★

But Pegleg didn't grow on Jesse. In fact, in the days that followed, the little dog became a big nuisance. For one thing, he was always staring at Jesse, following him around the room with those dark brown eyes. If Jesse so much as looked his way, Pegleg would start barking. And he wouldn't stop until Jesse came over to pet him. The barking got louder every time Jesse entered or left the room.

"Pegleg's in love with you," Tim teased. "And if you think you've got trouble *now*, just wait till he's on his feet again."

Jesse didn't have long to wait. Soon Pegleg was at his heels all the time, and his funny, hobbling walk didn't slow him down at all. It seemed that every

time Jesse turned around he was tripping over the pup.

Jesse hardly had a minute alone with Ginger anymore. One morning he was determined to spend some time with her before breakfast, but Pegleg kept licking his face. Finally, Jesse opened the door and pointed. "Out!" he told the little dog.

Pegleg slunk outside and hobbled down the front steps. But a moment later he put his paws on the windowsill and pressed his nose against the screen. And then, just to make his point, he began to bark louder than ever.

Jesse gritted his teeth. "What am I going to do with you?" he scolded, but he couldn't help smiling.

Pegleg barked some more in reply. He cocked his head and looked at Jesse.

Just then Joey, the farm's trainer, stormed in from the stable. "Will you keep that dog quiet?" he snapped. "He's driving the horses crazy — especially Glory!"

Pegleg scampered back inside before the door slammed shut. When Joey spun around to face him, the dog jumped back.

"Hey, can't you ever be quiet?" Joey yelled at Pegleg. Then he turned and looked at Jesse. "I don't understand it," he went on in a calmer voice. "I really don't. I know he can't help the way he *looks*, but what about the way he *sounds?* Why does he have to be so loud?"

Joey shook his head, then took another look at Pegleg and began to laugh. Jesse couldn't help laughing either, but he felt a little guilty.

For once Pegleg didn't pay any attention to Jesse. He was busy sniffing Ginger beneath the kitchen table. Ginger growled and charged at him. Pegleg hobbled away and flopped down on the floor just as Gran walked in to check some muffins in the oven.

"Problems?" Gran said.

"You're not kidding," Jesse told her. "This dog" — and he pointed to Pegleg — "is driving me crazy. He doesn't stop barking for a minute. He's making Ginger's life miserable. And he's bothering Glory, too. Isn't that right, Joey?" The trainer nodded.

"I'm sorry to hear that," Gran told Joey. Then, turning to Jesse, she said, "But it does make what I've got to tell you a lot easier."

"What's the matter?" Jesse asked.

"Gramp and I have been discussing the dog situation around here," Gran said, "and we think it's getting a bit out of hand. Pegleg's wound is healing nicely, and Ginger's cut is already mended. So there's really no reason for either of them to be here — especially in the house."

Gran caught sight of Jesse's stricken expression and gave him a quick hug. "Now don't you get all upset," she said. "Gramp and I both know how much you've always wanted a dog of your own. And we don't see any reason why you shouldn't have one. *One,*" she repeated as a big grin flashed across Jesse's face.

25

"We were afraid it was going to be tough for you to choose between the two dogs," Gran said, "seeing how fond of Ginger you've grown — and how fond of *you* Pegleg's grown! But from what you were just saying, I guess you've already made your choice. Isn't that so?"

Jesse hesitated.

"I know who *I'd* choose," Joey put in. "Don't I, girl?" He leaned over to pet Ginger. Jesse did, too. Joey gave Jesse a friendly punch on the arm before he headed toward the door.

"Jesse?" Gran said as soon as Joey was gone.

Jesse looked at her. "What?" He felt as if a giant thundercloud were hanging over him.

"You didn't answer my question. Isn't Ginger the dog you want?"

Of course she is! The words were on the tip of Jesse's tongue. But for some reason he couldn't say them.

"Jesse?" Gran prompted. When he

still didn't answer, she reached out and patted his head. "Well, there's no need to choose right this minute," she said. "It's an important decision.

"But in the meantime," Gran added, "you'll have to do something about Pegleg's barking. And let's be sure he stays downstairs at night. It's not fair to let him get too comfortable here if you're not going to be keeping him. Is that understood, young man?"

Jesse wriggled in his chair. "Understood," he muttered.

Jesse couldn't help feeling sorry for Pegleg. The little dog still wasn't used to getting around on just three legs. But how could Gran have even imagined he'd pick Pegleg over Ginger? Jesse wondered. And why was he even thinking about it? The kids at school would think Pegleg was silly-looking. They'd call him names. They'll call me names, too, he thought.

Jesse felt his shoulders slump. What

was he waiting for? His mind was made up, wasn't it? Why didn't he just tell Gran and get it over with?

He *would* tell her. He'd give Gran his decision right then and there. But as he jumped to his feet, he heard his grandmother say, "Now who can that be?"

Jesse walked over to the sink, where Gran was looking out the window. Pegleg was already by the door, barking at a bright red van that was pulling into the driveway.

Hastily, Gran took the muffins from the oven. She tested one with a toothpick, then put the pan on the rack to cool. As she went to the door, Jesse and Pegleg were right behind her. The little dog couldn't stop barking.

"No speak!" Jesse ordered. He'd read about that command in a dog-training book. Much to Jesse's surprise, Pegleg stopped and stayed quiet, even when a total stranger climbed out of the van.

The man was tall, tan, and nicely dressed. Right away Jesse noticed there was a gold pen sticking out of his shirt pocket.

"My name is Alan Arnold," the man introduced himself with a smile. Gran shook the hand he offered her. "This may sound odd," he went on in a soft voice, "but I feel as if I already know you."

Gran stiffened. "Know me?" she said.

"Yes," Alan Arnold replied. "You and River Oaks, that is. I'm a photographer — and your son Walt and I are friends. He and your daughter-in-law must have told me a hundred stories about this place. Now that I'm in town for a while, I thought I'd come by and see it for myself. I hope you don't mind."

Gran's face warmed. "Of course not," she said. "As soon as my husband gets back from the hardware store, I'll have him give you a tour."

"Oh, no," Alan Arnold answered. "I couldn't ask you to — "

"Nonsense," Gran broke in. "You're a friend of the family — isn't that right?"

"Well, yes," Alan Arnold said.

Jesse frowned. "I never heard my parents talk about you," he said.

"You're pretty young," Arnold told Jesse, bending down to pat his shoulder. Jesse drew back, but the man went right on speaking. "Maybe you were asleep when they mentioned my name."

Jesse turned away and looked at Ginger. All this time, she'd been dozing in a patch of sunlight. But not Pegleg. He hadn't taken his eyes off Alan Arnold. Gran hadn't noticed that. And there was something else she hadn't noticed. The entire time Alan Arnold had been talking, Pegleg — deep in his throat — had been growling at him.

Chapter Four

— ◆ —

The Suspicious Stranger

The next morning Jesse came downstairs early. Ginger was right behind him. As soon as he saw Jesse, Pegleg jumped up from his cushion and hobbled over to greet him.

"What's going on?" Jesse asked Tim and Arden. They were sitting at the breakfast table with big grins on their faces.

"Hey!" Jesse cried when they didn't answer. "What's the big secret?"

"Gran got a call this morning," Arden said.

"From who?" Jesse asked. "I didn't hear the phone ring."

"Maybe you were in the shower," said Arden.

"Fat chance," Tim said.

Jesse felt his cheeks getting hot. "Cut it out," he told Tim. "I don't hear *you* in the shower more than once or twice a year."

Arden scowled at Jesse. "*You* cut it out," she said. "Do you want to hear who called or don't you?"

"I want to," Jesse said. But deep inside he wasn't at all sure he did. He had a funny feeling. . . .

"It was Mr. Pierpont, the director of the Sunshine Bird Sanctuary," Arden went on. "You remember him, Jesse — Gran's old friend. We met him the last time we were here."

Jesse nodded. "Anyway," Arden said, "he invited Tim and me to come up there and help rescue birds."

"There's been an oil spill up the coast," Tim explained as he took his spoon and dish to the sink. "The oil got into the sea birds' feathers, and now a lot of the birds can't fly. We're going to help clean them up."

"Just you guys?" Jesse asked.

Arden shook her head no. "Some other kids, too," she said. "Ones that are interested in helping animals."

Jesse gulped. He was interested in helping animals. He really was. "I want to go, too," he blurted out. And when no one answered, he said, "How long will you be gone?"

"Two or three days," Tim said.

"We're leaving tomorrow!" Arden exclaimed. She looked as if she couldn't wait to go.

Jesse felt terrible. It seemed as if everyone were leaving him. He jumped up from the table and ran out of the house, Pegleg at his heels.

Gran was watering the flowers in the front yard. She put out her arm so Jesse wouldn't run past her. "Whoa there!" she said.

Jesse turned his head away. He could tell what was coming. Gran was going to try to make him feel better. But he didn't *want* any sympathy. Not right now.

"Please," Jesse whispered.

Gran smiled. "Why don't you take Pegleg for a walk?" she suggested. "You can go outside the farm so his barking won't disturb the other animals."

Jesse brightened. He reached down and played with Pegleg's ears. "I'll take Ginger, too," he said. He turned to call her, but the setter had already gone back inside.

Pegleg didn't need an invitation. He couldn't wait to get going. In fact, Jesse had to hurry to keep up with him. When they turned onto the town road, Pegleg picked up the pace even more. It always surprised Jesse how well Pegleg could get along on three and a half legs. Before he knew it, they were almost at the Martins' house.

Now it was Jesse who was in a hurry. He didn't want to meet the rude boy with the Mets cap Gramp and he had seen the other day. But, as usual, the little dog had a mind of his own. He tugged on the leash and dragged Jesse down the Martins' driveway.

Oh, well, the boy probably wasn't even home, Jesse thought as he tried to pull Pegleg back. But no such luck. There he was, lying in a hammock right in the front yard. And close up, he looked much bigger than he had from the truck.

Jesse's stomach was flip-flopping, but he got up enough nerve to walk toward the hammock. "Hello," he said.

The boy grunted. He barely glanced up from the book he was reading.

Jesse introduced himself. It seemed like years before the boy responded. "Zack Martin," he said, still reading. But when Pegleg sniffed him, he let his arm dangle and stroked the wagging tail.

Jesse pointed at Zack's book. "What's that?" he asked.

Zack glared as if Jesse were a pesky fly. "It's a book," he said. "What did you think it was?"

Jesse flushed. "I know it's a *book,*" he said. "But what *kind?*"

Zack sighed and held up the book. "It's a mystery — *The Case of the Green-eyed Cat.*"

"I read a mystery once," Jesse told him. "I liked it."

"That's nice," Zack said. Then he gave Pegleg a pat and buried his nose back in the book.

Jesse waited a minute before he tried again. "How long have you lived in this house?" he asked. There was an uncomfortable pause.

"I don't live here," Zack finally said. "I'm visiting my mother. She just moved here."

"Where's your father?"

"In New York."

"Is that where you live?" Jesse asked. Zack nodded.

Jesse took a deep breath. "I guess your mom and dad are divorced."

"Yeah," Zack said. "They're divorced."

"That's rough," Jesse said.

Zack shrugged. "I guess so."

"Well . . ." Jesse said. "I guess I'll go home now."

Again Zack shrugged.

Jesse sighed and turned to go.

"Hey," Zack called after him.

Jesse froze. "What?"

"Don't forget your dog."

Jesse looked back. Pegleg was still sitting by Zack's hammock.

"Come!" Jesse said, and Pegleg came. As they walked off, he heard Zack say, "That's some pup you've got there. But what happened to his leg?"

"He got into a fight with an alligator," Jesse said.

"Too bad. He's a cute pup," Zack answered. Jesse glanced at Pegleg. The dog looked as goony as ever. What was Zack talking about?

Jesse was just about to turn onto the road when he noticed a flash of color that seemed completely out of place in the dense green landscape. A bright red van was parked on the far edge of the Martins' property — right next to River Oaks.

Jesse saw it tucked away behind a cluster of dwarf cypresses. Alan Arnold's van! What was it doing over there? Gramp had given Arnold a full tour of River Oaks the day before. The man hadn't said a thing about coming back.

Pegleg was staring at the van, too, his ears pricked up like two stiff triangles. His body quivered as he opened his mouth to bark.

"No speak!" Jesse ordered, ducking down behind a clump of half-grown wild pine. He could hardly believe his luck when Pegleg closed his mouth and lay down quietly beside him.

"Hey, what's going on?" Zack called from the hammock.

"Sssh!" Jesse said. At that moment he didn't care whether Zack liked him or not.

But Zack was already moving toward the clump of pines. Jesse put a finger to his lips and pointed urgently at the van. He motioned to Zack to get down.

Just then Alan Arnold came into sight. He was walking through the tall grass with a heavyset man dressed in jeans and a plaid shirt. The two men kept looking around nervously.

Alan Arnold lifted the large, black binoculars he carried and looked through them. He looked right at River Oaks. In the meantime, the heavyset man was

peering in the same direction, using a telescope he'd propped on a tripod. Every so often, he made notes on his pad.

Jesse couldn't take his eyes off them. He was staring so closely he didn't see the small lizard dart in front of him. But Pegleg did. When the lizard's bright red throat pouch began to swell, the dog barked shrilly. Before Jesse could say "No speak," Pegleg barked again, and then again.

Alan Arnold and his friend whirled around. The heavyset man swung the telescope. Jesse gasped. Then he pulled Zack and Pegleg even farther down behind the wild pine so they wouldn't be seen. But they *had* been seen — *all* of them. He was sure of it!

Chapter Five

A New Friend

If Alan Arnold and his companion had seen the boys, they didn't pay any attention to them. They got into their van and sped away.

"What was that all about?" Zack asked. "Who *were* those guys? And what were they doing on your grandparents' property?"

"Nothing good, I bet," Jesse said. And then he told Zack all about Arnold's visit the day before, including Pegleg's — and his own — instinctive distrust of the man who claimed to be a family friend.

"Hmmm." Zack stroked his chin as

if a beard were there. "A *real* mystery," he said.

Jesse grinned.

Zack shielded his eyes from the sun and looked at Jesse. "Exactly what do your grandparents do at their rescue farm?" he asked.

Jesse proudly told Zack about the huge number of animals his grandparents cared for. For a second, he almost felt as if it were *his* farm he was talking about.

"Once *I* rescued an animal," Zack said. "A turtle. It had stopped in the middle of a road. I knew it would be a goner if it stayed where it was.

"There was just one problem," Zack explained with a twinkle in his eye.

"What?"

"I had to grab the turtle fast," Zack said. "I couldn't tell which direction it had been going in because its head was tucked under its shell. One end looked pretty much like the other, so — "

"So you didn't know which side of the road to put it on!" Jesse cut in.

Zack cocked his finger at Jesse. "You got it!" he said.

"I hope you guessed right," Jesse giggled. "Imagine how long it would take the poor thing to cross back!"

"Believe me, I've thought about it," Zack said. He gave Jesse a friendly smile.

Jesse smiled back.

Zack rubbed at a spot on his sneaker. "Are *your* parents divorced?" he asked suddenly.

Jesse shook his head no.

"Do you have any brothers and sisters?" Zack asked.

"One of each."

"You're lucky," Zack said.

"Are you an only child?" Jesse asked. He couldn't imagine not having Tim and Arden.

"Yup," Zack told Jesse. He looked a little uncomfortable.

Jesse didn't know what to say. But Pegleg changed the subject by flopping down right on top of his foot. "Pegleg!" he groaned. "That's my shoe, not a chair."

Zack laughed. "Dum-tee-dum-tee-dum," he teased the little dog.

"You sound as dopey as Pegleg looks," Jesse told him.

Zack threw a fake punch.

"Hey!" Jesse picked up the Mets cap that had fallen out of Zack's pocket and handed it back to the older boy.

"You play baseball?" Zack asked.

"Some," said Jesse. "I like to pitch."

"I'm a catcher," Zack said.

"Do you have an extra glove?" Jesse asked him.

"I could open up a sporting goods store!" Zack said just as his mother called to him from the doorway. "Wouldn't you know," he grumbled. "I finally find someone to pitch to me, and I have to go in. We'll play ball another time," he told Jesse. "Meanwhile," he added, as he slowly headed toward the house, "if you ever need any help with that mystery of yours, you know where to find me."

When Jesse came in for supper that night, Gran and Gramp hardly seemed to notice him. They were too busy talking about Frisky the mink.

"Did he seem sick this morning?" Gran asked Tim.

"I don't think so," Tim said. "But I was so excited about the trip to the bird sanctuary tomorrow. Maybe I wasn't paying enough attention."

Gran patted Tim's arm. "Don't worry," she said. "You usually notice everything. Everyone slips up once in a while."

"What's wrong with Frisky?" Arden asked.

"He's got a fever," Gramp replied, "and Gran and I have no idea what's causing it." Gramp sighed deeply. "There seem to be an awful lot of problems at River Oaks lately," he said.

Jesse knew Gramp was thinking about the town houses. Gently he put his hand on his grandfather's shoulder. This probably wasn't the time to bring up Alan Arnold, he thought. No one was in a "pay attention" mood. Still. . . .

"Gramp?" Jesse said quietly.

"What is it?" Gramp said.

Jesse took a deep breath. "Remember that boy we passed on the road last week? The one with the baseball cap?"

"Sure," Gramp said. "He was going into the Martins' place."

Jesse nodded. "I met him today, Gramp. His name is Zack. Pegleg and I were over at his house and we saw something really — "

"How old is Zack?" Tim interrupted.

"About twelve, I guess," Jesse said.

"Then what's he doing with a squirt like you?" Tim poked Jesse with his elbow.

Jesse fumed. Couldn't his brother see he had something important to say? "Anyway, Gramp — " he tried again.

"What, Sport?" Gramp said as he got up to help Gran clear the table. "Finished with your chicken?" he asked Arden, reaching for her plate.

"Uh-huh. Dinner was great." Arden smiled a thank you at her grandmother.

"Hey! *I* heated the oil! *I* made the batter!" Thomas Quinn's voice was lively again.

"Gramp, you're too much," Tim laughed just as Jesse surprised everyone — including himself — by opening up his mouth and yelling, "Won't anyone *listen* to me?" And while they all stared in silence, he said quickly, "Zack and I saw Alan Arnold today."

"You did?" Arden raised her eyebrows. "Where?"

Gran put away the bowl she was drying and sat back down at the table.

"On the edge of our property!" Jesse exclaimed.

"So what?" Tim said. "Mr. Arnold really liked the farm. He probably just wanted another look at it." He shrugged. "What's so terrible about that?"

"Tim's right," Gramp pointed out.

"Remember, Alan Arnold is a friend of your parents. He'd be more curious about the farm than a regular tourist might be." Gramp's eyes softened. "Doesn't that make sense?" he asked.

Jesse shook his head from side to side. "I've never even *heard* of Alan Arnold."

"Come on, Jess," Arden said impatiently. "You're only seven. Mom and Dad could have met Alan Arnold before you were even born!"

"Right," Tim put in. "I'm sure they have lots of friends we don't know about."

Jesse bristled. "You and Arden weren't there when Mr. Arnold came to the farm yesterday," he said. "You didn't hear how Pegleg kept growling at him."

"Neither did I," Gran said gently. "And I *was* there, Jesse."

"You were busy talking!" Jesse said shrilly. Why wouldn't anyone believe him?

Gran started to say something, but she got up instead and reached for

49

Frisky's chart. Soon her head was bent over the notes, and she seemed to be deep in thought.

"What were you going to say?" Jesse asked her.

Gran peered over the rims of her glasses. "Well," she said finally, "I guess I was going to ask you when you had your change of heart."

"What do you mean?" Jesse asked.

"I was just wondering," Gran said. "Since when do you put so much stock in what Pegleg does? You're always talking about how dumb he is."

Jesse gulped. "That's not true!" he protested. But in his heart he knew it was.

That night Jesse went to bed early. As usual, Ginger came upstairs with him. Minutes later she was sound asleep at the foot of his bed.

But Jesse couldn't sleep. He scrunched his pillow over his head and squeezed it hard to stop the thoughts that were buzzing through his mind. It seemed like hours before he finally fell asleep.

Jesse woke up suddenly during the night and blinked in the darkness. He felt a gentle breath on his neck, and then a rough tongue swept across his cheek.

For a minute Jesse was confused. It couldn't be Ginger — she was still snuggled up at his feet. There was only one other possibility.

"Pegleg, you sneak!" Jesse tried not to giggle as he scolded the dog. "You know you're not supposed to be up here!"

Pegleg moved closer and nuzzled Jesse's ear.

"Don't!" Jesse said. But he was really laughing now.

Then he stopped as a strange glow caught his eye. The moon was shining in on Pegleg, glinting off the dog's front paw. There was something metallic tucked beneath it.

Jesse gently moved the paw aside and found an old mousetrap on the bed.

"Thanks, Santa," he whispered before laying back on his pillow.

With Pegleg curled up by his head and Ginger snoring peacefully at his feet, Jesse once more found himself wide-awake.

What should he do? Which dog should he choose? For the first time he really wasn't sure. He wasn't sure at all. He'd told Ginger that he wanted her forever. But now. . . .

He turned his pillow over, looking for the coolest spot to rest his head. It was hard to choose between two living things. Soon he wouldn't have Pegleg anymore. Or he wouldn't have Ginger.

And there was something else to think about: Soon — very soon — one of these dogs wouldn't have *him!*

Chapter Six

————— ◆ —————

Tim and Arden
Take Off

"I see you had *two* guests in your room last night," Gran said first thing the next morning. She was standing at the bottom of the stairs, looking up at Jesse, Ginger, and Pegleg.

As Jesse opened his mouth to explain, Gran cut him off.

"No, don't say a word," she said.

Jesse waited for her to smile, but her mouth stayed in a straight line.

"Jesse, I *told* you," Gran said. "I don't want Pegleg upstairs until you decide which dog you're keeping. And you have to choose between them soon, Jesse. You absolutely have to."

Jesse had never seen Gran look so stern. He could tell it wasn't easy for her, asking him to give an animal away. But much as he hated to admit it, he understood the problem. If she kept every dog that came to River Oaks, there'd be a hundred animals in the house — and no room for any people. Unfortunately, that didn't make his choice any easier.

★ ★ ★ ★

At breakfast, Jesse stared blankly into his cereal.

"What's the matter?" Arden asked. "Dog trouble?"

Jesse nodded fiercely.

Arden touched his arm. "Don't worry," she said. "Gran will find a good home for the dog you don't keep."

Jesse smiled at her. Arden and Gran always seemed to know what he was thinking.

"Gran will *try* to, you mean," Tim said. He reached for the butter. Then he glanced at Pegleg. "Why would anyone take in a three-legged mutt when they could have a perfect, purebred dog like Ginger?"

Arden glared at Tim.

"What?" he said to her, leaning back in his chair. "You act so smart, Arden," he said, "but you know I'm right."

"You're wrong," Arden said. "Not everyone cares so much about what a dog *looks* like."

"Just a minute," Gran interrupted. "Maybe Tim didn't need to say what he did, but he's not completely wrong."

Jesse looked at Gran. Did she think no one would take Pegleg? Would she give Pegleg to the pound if no one wanted him? He couldn't think of anything more horrible.

Jesse knew he'd never forgive himself if that happened. He knew he'd never be able to enjoy Ginger. But if he picked Pegleg, that might be horrible, too. What if Pegleg wasn't the dog he really wanted? Suddenly, his head began to throb.

"That's no wonder," Gran said when he told her. "You have a difficult choice to make."

"Pegleg would *hate* the pound," Jesse said, sneaking a look at his grandmother. "He'd bark all the time. Everyone would get mad at him."

"You don't really think I'd send him there, do you?" Gran said. "Even if it were hard to do, I'd find a good home for Pegleg — just like Arden said." Gran reached out and patted Jesse on the shoulder. "Okay?" she asked him.

Jesse nodded, but he still felt awful. He was relieved to see his grandfather coming in from the den.

"What's the matter, Sport?" Gramp said. "Is the family picking on you?"

Jesse smiled a little.

"That Alan Arnold fella just called," Gramp said cheerfully.

"Alan Arnold!" Jesse cried.

"What did Mr. Arnold want?" Gran asked.

"To thank me for his tour around the farm," Gramp told her.

"He already thanked you," Jesse pointed out with a frown.

"Jesse, please. . . ." Gran's voice sounded tight.

Gramp reached for a piece of toast. "Listen to your grandmother," he said. "We don't have any time to waste arguing this morning. Tim and Arden have to get ready. Their plane for the Sunshine Bird Sanctuary leaves in a couple of hours.

"By the way," Gramp said to Jesse, "Mr. Arnold asked me to say 'hi' to you."

"See, Jess?" Tim said. "Mr. Arnold didn't do anything wrong. If he had, he wouldn't have called us."

"That's what *you* think," Jesse muttered.

No one said anything.

Jesse leaned forward and looked straight at Gramp. "Did Mr. Arnold tell you he was with someone?" he said, his voice shaking. "Did he mention his tough-looking friend?"

"Why, no," Gramp said. He glanced at Gran and for a moment they both looked uneasy. Then Gramp's face relaxed into a smile as he leaned toward Jesse. "Tell me the truth," he said. "You *look* like a regular kid, but you're really a private detective, aren't you?"

Jesse didn't smile back. Maybe his

mind *was* playing tricks on him.

But no, he decided. He wasn't being silly, and he wasn't imagining things, either. Alan Arnold was up to something!

"Hey, Tim," Jesse said. "What time are you leaving?" He'd been trailing after his brother and sister since breakfast. Now he and Tim were helping Arden search her room for a lost pair of sneakers.

"The plane leaves at ten-thirty," Tim said. "But we have to be at the airport a half-hour early."

Arden stood in the middle of the room, hands on her hips. "Now where could they be?" she muttered to herself.

Kneeling down on the floor, Arden lifted her bedspread ruffle and peeked beneath it. Then she stuck her arm under the bed and fumbled around.

"Here they are!" she said. She got up and crammed the sneakers into her duffel bag.

"Hurry up," Tim said. "We're going to be late."

"I don't see why I can't go with you," Jesse said.

"You're just a little kid."

"So?" Jesse thrust his chin out at Tim and said, "I'm still a person, aren't I? How big do you have to be to carry a little bird?"

Arden spoke gently. "I guess some people think you have to be all grown-up to be good at anything."

"*You're* not grown-ups," Jesse said. "You're not even teenagers yet!"

"We're older than you are," Tim said impatiently.

Jesse didn't say anything. All his words were stuck in a lump in his throat. He was going to miss his brother and sister a lot.

Arden sneezed.

"Maybe you're getting sick!" Jesse said hopefully.

Arden blew her nose. "It's just the

dust," she said, "from under the bed."

Then Tim sneezed.

"*You* weren't under the bed!" Jesse exclaimed. His eyes swept to Arden then back again. "Maybe you two should stay home," he said. "You can never tell about colds."

Tim rolled his eyes. "If you don't stop bothering us, we're going to miss our plane," Tim said as he started down the stairs. "Hurry up, Arden," he called over his shoulder. "Jesse, stop acting like such a baby!"

Jesse felt as if Tim had knocked him over. Tears came to his eyes as he listened to his brother run down the stairs. Jesse knew Arden was staring at him, but he was too ashamed to look at her.

"Tim didn't mean it," Arden said.

"Yes he did."

"Believe me, Jess, we both think you're very grown-up — for your age. When I was seven I was still afraid of the dark. I wanted every light in the room on while I was falling asleep."

"I'm not afraid of the dark," said Jesse.

"I know you're not," Arden told him. Then she smiled and said, "Tim's lucky. When he acted like a baby, we were too young to notice."

"He *still* acts like a baby sometimes," Jesse said.

"You're right," Arden agreed, heading for the stairs. "We all do now and then. But don't feel bad. I'm sure Tim's sorry about what he said."

And sure enough, when they got outside, Tim was leaning against the jeep with an apologetic smile on his face. His bag was already in back. Gran and Gramp were sitting in the front seat.

"Hey, Jess," he said.

Jesse ducked his head down and didn't answer. "Come on!" he heard Tim call to Arden.

"Sorry the jeep's so small, Jesse," Gran said as Arden climbed into the backseat.

Gramp bent to look past Gran at Jesse. "There's always room for one more," he said. "Want to sit on my lap?"

"No. That's all right," Jesse said. He was standing right beside Tim, but refused to look at him. "I have to feed Mortie," he explained. "Then I'm going to take Pegleg for a walk."

"If you need anything," Gran said, "just ask Joey. He's in the tack room, polishing the saddles." She planted a kiss on Jesse's cheek before starting the engine.

"So long, Jesse," Arden called to him.

"Good-bye," Jesse called back. He was pleased to hear how steady his voice sounded. "You have a good time. Save a lot of birds."

"We will," Tim said, putting a hand on Jesse's shoulder.

Jesse glanced up at his older brother and then quickly looked away.

"Hey, don't be a grump," Tim said. "Look, I drew something for you." He held out a piece of paper. "I was going to wait and give it to you for your birthday, but this seems like as good a time as any."

Jesse tried to stay angry at Tim, but his curiosity got the better of him. "Let me see!" he said, snatching the paper from Tim's hand and unfolding it.

"Wow! Thanks!" he said when he saw what Tim had drawn.

Tim mussed Jesse's hair and climbed in next to Arden. "Ready for takeoff," he told Gran.

Jesse hardly saw the jeep leaving. He was too busy admiring Tim's sketch of him and Ginger and Pegleg. The picture showed Jesse laughing while the two dogs licked his cheeks. Beneath the drawing Tim had printed the words: EVERYBODY LOVES JESSE.

Chapter Seven

—◆—

Alan Arnold Returns

Jesse reached inside Mortie's cage and shook some seed into the bowl. The mynah bird flapped his wings and shifted from foot to foot.

"Thank you, Sport," Mortie squawked.

Jesse smiled. He'd worked hard teaching Mortie those words last week and was glad to see the bird still remembered them.

The mynah bird would echo almost anything anyone said, but he didn't always say the right thing at the right time. And he never was this polite! "Shut up," was his favorite expression, and he usually called Jesse "Shorty" instead of "Sport."

Jesse spent the next half hour trying to get Mortie to say, "Peanuts, please," but the bird was strangely silent. Jesse finally gave up and went inside to do his chores.

Pegleg shadowed him as usual, biting at the dish towel when Jesse dried the dishes, burrowing under the covers when he tried to make his bed. It was after eleven by the time Jesse finally finished and turned his full attention to the dog.

"Okay, boy," Jesse said. "We're going now." He reached behind Pegleg to where Ginger lay sleeping near the door and scratched the setter's back. "You, too, girl," he told her. Ginger opened one eye, then quickly closed it.

Meanwhile, Pegleg was already dancing around Jesse's feet. The little dog got tangled up in his leash, and his tail brushed across Ginger's face.

Ginger lifted her head, stretched lazily, and gave Pegleg a peevish glance. Then she sank down on the braided rug and her eyelids fluttered shut again. Jesse leaned over and patted Ginger's head. "I know just how you feel," he said. "Sometimes I wish Pegleg could exercise himself!"

The little dog barked, and Jesse laughed. "Sorry, Pegleg," he said, clipping on the leash. "I didn't mean to hurt your feelings."

They left the sleeping Ginger and headed out. As they walked, Jesse let his mind wander. Tim and Arden's plane must have already taken off. Gran and Gramp weren't back from the airport yet. And Joey was down in the stable. Jesse realized that even though he was all alone, he felt better than he had in a long time. Maybe it was Mortie's thank-you — or, more likely, Tim's drawing. But today, all by himself, Jesse finally felt like *somebody*.

Jesse suddenly noticed that the wind was picking up. Dark clouds swept toward River Oaks from the Gulf of Mexico and erased the sunny skies. Far away, thunder boomed. Jesse began walking even faster. Gramp had warned him about Florida lightning. It could strike at any time near a storm.

"Yip! Yip! Yip!" Pegleg cried as he stumbled on a rock. Jesse dropped to his knees beside him.

"Poor pup," he crooned, stroking the little dog. "I won't walk so fast anymore. I promise."

The tip of Pegleg's tail wagged wildly as he got to his feet and licked Jesse's hand. Then he tilted his head to watch an armadillo go scooting up the road ahead of them and disappear behind a tree stump.

Jesse breathed in the sweet scent of orchids. A dragonfly whizzed by his ear, and he ducked. Then he stopped to watch a tree snail inch its way along a branch. A grasshopper was creeping along right behind, munching on the green leaves.

Jesse was glad that Gran and Gramp had taught him how to really see and smell and listen. He'd never paid much attention to nature until he came to the farm.

"Jesse!" An urgent cry interrupted his thoughts.

Jesse turned toward the road and thought he heard his name again over Pegleg's excited barking.

"No speak!" Jesse said, peering through the haze that was steaming off the blacktop. There was Zack running toward him, waving both hands.

Pegleg ran to greet the boy, and Jesse followed. Zack was panting when they reached him.

"What's happening?" Jesse asked.

"Hold on a minute," Zack said. He bent over to catch his breath before going on. "It's that guy again."

"What guy?" Jesse asked.

"Alan Arnold! Who else?" Zack tugged at Jesse. "Come *on*. Arnold and that other guy are nosing around your grandparents' property again," he said. "Let's go! What are you waiting for?"

Jesse couldn't speak. He didn't know what to say — or do. Should he run to the farm and let Gran and Gramp know what was going on? They should be home by now. But he wasn't exactly sure what *was* going on. Maybe he should go with Zack and try to find out what Alan Arnold and the other man were really up to! He gulped. What if he did the wrong thing and something awful happened?

It was Pegleg who suddenly made the decision for him. With his leash trailing along the road, the little dog charged toward Zack's house. Jesse raced after him, with Zack close behind.

"Pegleg," Jesse hissed, as quietly as he could so the men wouldn't hear him. Then louder, "Pegleg!"

Zack leaped ahead, scooped up the eager little dog, and dropped him into Jesse's arms. Then he marched along the shoulder of the road toward the pines on his mother's property — to the exact spot where Jesse had first seen Arnold's bright red van. And there, only a hundred feet or so away, stood Alan Arnold and his fat friend!

Jesse strained to see over a clump of scrub. Pegleg still quivered but didn't make a sound.

Suddenly Alan Arnold turned, and Jesse got a clearer view of his face. The friendly smile he'd worn for Gran was gone — and so was the soft voice.

"The farm's almost ours," Jesse heard Arnold say.

The wind shifted, carrying Arnold's voice closer. "All we have to do," he said, "is get the dumb animals off the land. And I know just how to do it," he gloated. "First, we — "

Trying to hear better, Jesse leaned so far forward that he almost fell into the scrub. But Arnold had turned away, and the rest of his words were lost in the wind.

Pegleg seemed determined to wriggle free, so Zack helped Jesse hold him. But neither boy could do anything about the dog's little yelps of protest. Jesse tensed, praying the men would leave before Pegleg drew their attention.

They did leave — and just in time. As Pegleg burst through the scrub to bark at the fading roar of Arnold's van, Jesse pushed himself to his feet.

"We've got to get back to River Oaks," he said. "I have to tell my grandparents what we just saw."

"And *heard,*" Zack said grimly.

"*Almost* heard, you mean," Jesse grumbled. "We still don't know what Alan Arnold's planning to do." He sighed. Things were getting awfully complicated!

"You think your grandparents will believe you?" Zack asked.

"They'll have to," Jesse shouted as

he started running. In a flash, Pegleg and Zack were by his side.

Jesse's heart sank when they reached the farm. "They're not *here!*" he cried, gaping at the spot where Gran's jeep should have been. From his cage nearby, Mortie let out a squawk.

"They'll be back," Zack said. "The airport isn't far. Maybe they stopped off for coffee or something. But while we're waiting" — Zack gestured toward the office — "let's get out of the heat."

Jesse ran his tongue over his dry lips and tried to smile. "Sure," he said. "I'll treat you to a glass of water."

"Thank you, Sport," Mortie screeched.

Jesse chuckled at the mynah bird. "I *fed* you already!" he said. "That bird thinks he's a pig," he joked. But Zack didn't answer.

When Jesse turned to see why his friend hadn't responded, he saw that Zack was already on the porch, his head bent over a piece of yellow paper.

Jesse walked toward him. "What's that?" he asked.

"A note," Zack said without raising his eyes. "It was tucked in the door frame."

"Who's it for?"

Zack finally looked up. "Your grandfather left it for you."

"What?" Jesse said. "Gramp wrote me a note? He and Gran were back here?"

Zack handed the paper to Jesse. "Look for yourself," he said.

Dear Jesse, Thomas Quinn had written. *Gran just got an emergency call from the chimp station. One of the males is running loose at the edge of the farm. Gran and I had to go look for him. Sorry we couldn't wait for you, but we'll be home as soon as we can.*

P.S., the note ended, *There's lemonade in the fridge. Help yourself.*

Jesse was still thirsty. But lemonade was the last thing he had on his mind. There was something about the note that didn't sound quite right. He read it over and over to see if he could put his finger on it.

Jesse was ready to admit that maybe he was being too suspicious when the shrill sound of the telephone made him drop the note.

"You sure are jumpy," Zack said, but Jesse was already running inside to answer it. And when he ran back out a few minutes later, he looked really worried.

"What's wrong?" Zack asked.

"That was my mother, calling from Africa," Jesse told him. "And guess what?" But he didn't wait for Zack to reply. "My parents don't have any friend named Alan Arnold. They never even *heard* of the guy!"

"Well, why are we just standing here?" Zack said. "We'd better go find your grandparents and tell them. How do you get there?"

"Where?"

"To the chimp station."

Jesse shook his head. "It's over that

way." He pointed to a dirt road that led deep into the farm. "About a mile or so."

Zack's eyes surveyed the swampy land nearby.

"What are you looking for?" Jesse asked. The expression on the older boy's face frightened him.

"A short cut," Zack said. He was already heading toward a narrow path that disappeared into the brush.

Jesse ran to catch up. "This isn't smart," he said. "I'm not even sure where the chimp station *is* exactly." He grabbed Zack's arm. "Why can't we wait here till Gran and Gramp get back? Or at least follow the dirt road and not some stupid path!"

Zack shook Jesse off and kept on walking. "What if your grandparents can't *find* the chimp?" he said. "What if there *is* no chimp? I mean, maybe it was Alan Arnold who made this 'emergency' call."

Jesse stuck to Zack like a shadow.

"Why would he do that?" he asked, glancing back uneasily. Already the path seemed to have closed up behind them.

"To get your grandparents far away from here," Zack replied.

"But why?"

"I don't know," Zack admitted. He motioned to Jesse. "Just come *on*."

Jesse ran ahead, blocking Zack's way. He blotted his damp forehead with the bottom of his T-shirt, then looked up at his friend. "You don't have any idea where you're going, do you?" he said.

Zack didn't say anything. He just swatted a mosquito and gave Jesse a dark look before moving on.

Jesse hurried to stay close and stumbled into a tree stump. "What's wrong with you, Zack?" he cried, rubbing his leg. "You're leading us straight into the middle of nowhere!"

Zack stopped walking and let out a deep sigh. "Listen, Half-pint," he said. "I know it's scary wandering around in this muck, but I have a strong feeling that something's wrong, and only your grandparents can set it right. Believe me, I'm not doing this for fun."

Jesse ducked as a big bee buzzed around his head. Luckily, it found a bright purple orchid in a tree above Zack and rested there. Jesse made a sour face, but trudged along behind Zack. "I just hope you know what you're doing," he mumbled.

He was thinking about something Gramp once told him: "People get in trouble," Gramp had said, "when they don't listen to what their hearts are telling them." But even though Jesse knew exactly what Gramp had meant, he continued to follow Zack.

With each step he took, Jesse felt more and more uneasy. He realized that he hadn't been listening to his heart at all. He'd been doing what Zack wanted him to do. That had seemed a lot easier than saying, No. I'm going to wait at home for Gran and Gramp. You go ahead if you want.

Jesse was about to say those words out loud when Pegleg began to bark.

Zack had stopped walking and was staring straight ahead.

"Terrific," he groaned.

"What's the matter?" Jesse said. And then he saw what Zack had just seen. His mouth dropped open and he groaned, too. The path they were on had come to a dead end. There was nothing ahead but a thick gnarl of ferns and young palms.

Some shortcut, Jesse almost said. But he wasn't all that sorry to see it. Now they'd *have* to turn back. Besides, Zack looked so unhappy, Jesse didn't have the heart to rub it in.

Jesse reached into his pocket and took out Gramp's handkerchief. He could feel a tickle starting behind his nose. But before he could sneeze, Pegleg sprang as high as his three good legs would take him and snatched the handkerchief from Jesse's hand.

"You give that back!" Jesse scolded.

"This is no time to be fooling around!"
He grabbed at the handkerchief. But
Pegleg hung on, growling happily.

Jesse sighed. He wasn't in the mood
for this. He had just marched a half mile
in the scorching heat.

"You can *have* the stupid handker-chief!" he said, suddenly letting go of it. Pegleg stumbled backward.

Zack couldn't help smiling as he caught the playful pup. "We might as well go back," he said to Jesse. "Maybe your grandparents are home by now."

Jesse nodded and turned back. At once he felt the wind shift. He breathed deeply. The air seemed hotter than ever. He scrunched up his nose and took another breath.

"Zack?" he said.

"What?"

"Do you smell what I smell?" Jesse asked. More than anything in the world, he wanted Zack to say no.

Chapter Eight

———•———

Fire!

"Smoke!" Zack cried, and Jesse felt his stomach tighten.

"You okay?" Zack asked.

Jesse didn't answer. He *wasn't* okay. Fire was the worst thing that could happen to an animal farm — the very worst thing.

Just a week ago he'd seen a really scary movie about a forest fire. Pine trees had shot from the ground like rockets, setting wooden buildings ablaze and scattering animals for miles around.

Now Jesse shut his eyes to blot out that picture. Even the thought of a fire made him sick. "Let's go back," he whispered hoarsely.

Jesse took one step, then stopped short. His heart sank as he looked around him. Suddenly every leaf, every stump, every tree looked exactly like every other.

Zack saw how scared Jesse was and said, "Calm down. Just calm down." But he didn't feel very calm himself. He had no idea which way was home!

While Pegleg played with Jesse's handkerchief, the two boys searched for tracks. Not too far back, Jesse remembered, he'd glanced behind and seen his footprints in a patch of mud. But there were no tracks now. It seemed as if the swamp had swallowed them up.

Just as both boys were about to panic, the sun sent a sliver of light through the shadows. And that's when Jesse saw it — the big, purple orchid. It seemed to be beckoning him. "Look!" he cried.

Zack followed Jesse's gaze, and then stared blankly at his friend. "Look?" he echoed. "At what? A *flower?* You must be kidding!" But Jesse was already dragging him through the undergrowth. Pegleg hobbled along behind.

"Hurry, you guys," Jesse urged. "I think I know where we are now."

Just beyond the tree where the orchid grew, the ground suddenly cleared. There were the footprints — and paw prints, too — Jesse remembered seeing. The boys stood for a moment, taking deep breaths. Then Jesse bolted for home.

Zack matched him stride for stride. "What are you going to do when you get back?" he gasped as they ran.

"I don't know!" Jesse answered. *"Something!"* he said, dodging a salamander. He raced even faster when he saw tiny licks of flame in the distance.

Thunderclouds were closing in. The smoke thickened. Jesse could hear restless animals in their compounds all over the farm. *Let Gran and Gramp be home!* he hoped as his footsteps thudded on the ground.

But they weren't. Jesse realized that the moment he saw the empty parking area in front of the office. At least Zack was with him. Zack could help him wet down the office and clinic so they wouldn't burn. And he could help figure out a way to protect the animals. Of course, they'd call the fire department first thing.

Jesse's mind was racing like a runaway car. Suddenly he felt more hopeful. He —

"Wait up!" Zack called, and Jesse skidded to a stop.

Zack was as pale as a ghost. "I just remembered something," he panted.

"What?"

"My mother," Zack said. "She worked late last night. I think she's still asleep."

"You'd better call her," Jesse said, urging his friend into the office.

Zack balked. "Her phone's not connected yet," he said.

Jesse felt all hope fading as he shoved his friend away from him. "You'd better go home!" he told Zack fiercely. "If your mother's sleeping, she might not smell the smoke. And the way the wind's blowing it around, the fire could spread awfully fast. What are you waiting for? Your mother needs you."

Zack ran a few steps, then halted. Slowly he turned back to Jesse. "It isn't right," he said.

"What isn't right?"

"Leaving you. You're just a little kid. You need me, too."

Jesse's heart beat faster, but he tried to smile bravely. "I'll be all right," he said. "Joey's in the stable. He'll know what to do."

Zack gave Jesse a searching look and sighed. "Okay," he said, "you win — but *only*," he joked, "because Pegleg's here to help you."

"Pegleg," Jesse grunted. The little dog looked up then and cocked his head, Gramp's handkerchief still hanging from his mouth.

Jesse brightened suddenly. What was it the hiker had said? *Pegleg has a nose like a bloodhound!* Maybe, Jesse thought, just maybe. . . .

He yanked the handkerchief from Pegleg's mouth and dangled it just out of reach until the little dog was dancing for it.

"What are you *doing?*" Zack said. "The whole place is about to burn up, and you're playing with your dog!"

But Jesse didn't even seem to hear Zack. All his energy was zeroed in on Pegleg. "Take the handkerchief to Gramp," he said urgently. "Go! Go to Gramp!"

"Are you out of your *mind?*" Zack said.

Maybe he *was* out of his mind, Jesse suddenly thought. What chance did Pegleg really have of getting help?

Zack was shaking his head. "Jesse! Stop him! Please!" he cried as Pegleg ran off toward the swamp. When Zack spoke again his voice was low and hollow. "What's wrong with you? Pegleg's just a little dog. He'll never make it."

Jesse's heart sank. What had he been thinking of? "Pegleg!" he called. "Pegleg! Come back!" But the wind was too strong. His voice didn't carry.

Jesse felt a light touch on his arm. "I gotta go," Zack said, and his voice was calmer. "Call the fire department, okay? Or have Joey do it."

Jesse nodded solemnly.

"You've got time," Zack told him, leaning away now, ready to run. "You'll be all right." And he was gone.

Jesse shivered. *You really think so?* he wanted to shout. But instead, his eyes burning with tears — or was it the smoke? — he ran to the stable.

"Joey!" he called. "Joey! Where are you?" Inside the stable, one of the horses reared in its stall while Glory whinnied nervously. But Joey didn't answer, even when Jesse called again and again. "Easy, Glory," Jesse said. "I'll find Joey for you."

Jesse went outside and circled the stable, but the trainer was nowhere to be found. By the time Jesse ran back to the office, his heart was pounding with fear and exhaustion. The room was hazy now, not sunny. It had never seemed so big, or so still.

Today of all days, Gran's desk was a total mess. Jesse dug through one pile of papers after another. It seemed like hours before he finally found Gran's phone book.

With shaky fingers Jesse dialed the volunteer fire department. He gave his name and explained the situation to the man who answered.

"Yes, *Quinn!*" he repeated. "I'm at the River Oaks Animal Rescue Farm. Right. On the town road. Hurry! Please!"

Jesse hung up the receiver and stood perfectly still for a moment as he tried to decide what to do next. Part of him wanted to rush outside to see how fast the fire was spreading. The other part wanted to do nothing but curl up and hide. If only Ginger and Pegleg were with him — he'd hold them so tight!

Where *was* Ginger? Jesse wondered suddenly. He hadn't seen the setter since he and Pegleg had left her napping. "Ginger!" he called as he ran through the house trying to find her.

Then Jesse thought he heard someone calling *him,* and he dashed outside. But no one was there. "Hello?" he said, swallowing smoke and coughing. And then, "Gramp!" he shouted in relief as he saw his grandfather running toward him.

Jesse flew into Gramp's embrace. He couldn't hold him close enough. "You're back!" he cried. "I thought you'd never come! How did you — "

The next thing Jesse knew he was bouncing along in his grandfather's arms as Gramp raced away from the office. "Stay put," Gramp ordered, plunking Jesse down on the edge of the black-topped parking lot. "There's less smoke here. I'll be back as soon as I call the fire department," Gramp promised. And then he vanished again.

"Gramp! Wait!" Jesse shouted. "I already called!" But he knew Gramp couldn't hear him.

Jesse rubbed his eyes. Even in the parking lot, the smoke was pretty thick. But now Jesse realized there was actually a lot more smoke than fire. Still, he was all alone again.

Jesse almost jumped out of his skin at the sound of footsteps crunching behind him — until he saw that the arms hugging him close belonged to his grandmother.

"Oh, Jesse," Gran was saying. "Thank goodness you're all right. But where's Joey? Why isn't he here with you?"

Jesse felt relief wash through him. "I don't know where Joey is," he told his grandmother, "but I'm all right. I'm *more* than all right now!" And suddenly he was.

Gran straightened up and began pulling Jesse toward the garden shed. "Let's get some buckets and hoses," she said. "We've got to make sure the fire doesn't spread. Why don't we just — ?"

But a great clap of thunder stopped Gran in her tracks and drowned out the rest of her words. "Well, isn't that something," Gran remarked, holding out her hand.

"Rain!" Jesse shouted. He tilted his face and let the cool drops fall on his hot cheeks.

"It's really coming down, too!" Gran said happily.

Just then, Joey came stumbling toward the shed, red-faced and breathless. "I'm so sorry . . ." he gasped. "I ran out of polish for the saddles and went to the Van Vreens to borrow some more . . . Vince and I got talking and. . . ." Joey shook his head. "Really," he said, looking straight into Gran's eyes, "there wasn't any smoke when I went over there. You have to believe me."

Gran pulled Jesse under an overhang out of the rain. "Of course I believe you," she told Joey.

"So do I," Gramp said, coming up behind them. "The wind must have shifted. We didn't see or smell the smoke, either." He gave the trainer a stern look before adding, "But that's not the point. You should have been here anyway — fire or no fire. Jesse might have needed you. But I'm glad you're okay. We were worried about you, too!"

"And where have *you* been?" Gran said to Gramp as he made room for himself and Joey under the overhang.

"*Somebody* had to call the fire department," Gramp said brusquely. "I had a hard time getting through." He knelt in front of Jesse, his voice going soft as he gazed proudly at his grandson. "But," he added, "it seems somebody got through before me."

"Hey, listen," Jesse said. Down the road came the old town fire truck. Everyone could hear the loud, clanging noise it made as it raced toward the farm.

Gramp got to his feet. "That's the sweetest sound I ever heard," he said with a twinkle in his eye. "But they're a little late, aren't they?"

As he reached out to hug Gran and Jesse, Gramp suddenly noticed that his grandson still looked upset. "What's wrong, Sport?" he said. "There's nothing to worry about now. The rain's just about put the fire out, and the whole family's safe and sound."

Jesse felt tears welling up in his eyes again. "No, it's not," he said, his voice cracking. "Ginger's still missing. And wh-what about Pegleg?" he stammered as the tears threatened to fall.

Gran threw her head back and laughed. "Oh, my goodness," she said, mussing Jesse's damp hair. "I'm sorry. In all the excitement I almost forgot about them."

Gran led Jesse to the far side of the parking lot. There, inside the jeep, a familiar face was pressed against the rain-streaked window.

"Pegleg!" Jesse cried. The little dog leaped up and made the horn beep. "Pegleg *did* find you!" Jesse said to his grandfather.

"You bet he did!" Gramp opened the jeep door and Pegleg threw himself at Jesse.

"Good boy," Jesse said, giving the dog a big hug. He was almost afraid to ask the next question, but he had to know.

"What about Ginger?" Jesse said hesitantly.

Joey had been looking behind the backseat. Now he pulled it forward and pointed. And there was Ginger, crouched underneath it, her tail thumping against the car floor.

"Aw, Ginger," Jesse said, reaching in for her. "Were you scared? Well, so was I. But I'm not scared anymore."

"We're lucky we got away with nothing but smoke damage," Gramp said at supper that night. "You never can tell what will happen when lightning strikes."

Jesse made a face. "It was Alan Arnold who struck," he said, "not lightning."

Gramp gave Jesse a skeptical look, but Tansy Quinn spoke up for her grandson. "I'm beginning to think Jesse may have been right all along," she said. "Did you forget the wild chimp chase?" And turning to Jesse, she explained, "We phoned the chimp station after the firemen left, and they didn't even know what we were talking about. The chimp had been there all along."

As soon as Gran said the word *phoned,* Jesse suddenly remembered his mother's call. In all the excitement he'd forgotten to tell Gran and Gramp that neither one of his parents had ever even *heard* of Alan Arnold!

Chapter Nine

The Big Clue

The next day Jesse went over to Zack's house to give his friend the latest news.

"It's so quiet now," Zack said from his usual place in the hammock. "It's hard to believe that there was so much excitement yesterday."

Jesse didn't answer. His eyes were fixed on the creek across the road. A great blue heron was wading there, patiently waiting for a fish.

"That's some bird," Zack said when Jesse pointed it out.

Jesse nodded. Then he sighed. "It *is* pretty quiet now," he said. "It almost seems as if the fire never happened."

"I can still smell the smoke a little," Zack said. He made himself more comfortable. "And a lot of trees are pretty black."

Jesse nodded slowly. He was thinking about how much worse it could have been.

"Orrk!" the heron screeched suddenly. It spread its wings and flew to another wading spot.

Zack sat up. "I wonder what scared it."

There was a sudden rustling in the scrub palm near the road. *"Guess,"* Jesse said, as Pegleg came hobbling toward them.

"Look!" Zack said. "Pegleg's brought you something."

"Two things!" Jesse laughed as a whistle and a pinecone were dropped at his feet.

Zack laughed, too. "Pegleg looks great today," he said. "What did you do to him?"

"I gave him a bath — Ginger, too.

They really smelled from all that smoke. Ginger's still home drying."

Zack grinned. "I bet Ginger wasn't sorry you left without her. Pegleg's probably not her favorite companion."

"Sometimes Pegleg isn't *my* favorite companion," Jesse said. He thought for a minute, looking at the little dog. "But I have to admit he did okay yesterday."

"*Okay?*" Zack said.

Jesse grinned and ruffled Pegleg's ears.

"I've got something for you, too," Zack said, reaching underneath the hammock and dropping two baseball gloves and an old baseball in front of Jesse.

Jesse's eyes lit up.

"I had a hunch you'd be coming over today," Zack told him with a gleam in his eyes. He picked up the ball and catcher's mitt. "So," he said, winding up like a big-league pitcher, but he stopped short before tossing the ball to Jesse. "There's just one thing I don't understand," he said. "How did Alan Arnold know so much about your parents?"

100

Jesse had picked up the pitcher's glove and was backing up, too. His voice got slightly louder as he explained about the newspaper article on his parents Gramp and he had seen.

"I saw that article the day I first saw you from Gramp's truck," Jesse called out. "The day you didn't smile at me."

"Sorry about that," Zack said. He threw Jesse the ball and Pegleg tried to get it. "I have trouble meeting new people — even half-pints like you. I guess I'm kind of shy."

All the time the boys were throwing the ball to one another, Pegleg raced back and forth trying to catch it. Finally Zack flopped down on the grass.

Rolling onto his stomach, he toyed with the pinecone Pegleg had delivered. "Well," he said, "it looks like we were right all along. Alan Arnold really *did* start that fire!"

"Uh-huh," Jesse told him. "Even Gramp thinks so now."

"There's only one thing I don't understand," Zack said. "Why would Alan Arnold set fire to land he wanted to buy?" He sat up suddenly. "Unless he thought your grandparents would sell him the land cheap — because it was no good to them anymore. Then he could put up his town houses — "

" — and sell them for a lot of money," Jesse finished. "At least that's what my grandparents think."

"Whew!" Zack shook his head in amazement. "But why did Arnold pretend to be a friend of your family?"

"That's easy!" Jesse said. "He needed to get a real good look at the land — and he didn't want anyone to know what he was doing."

"And you figured that out by yourself, Mr. That's Easy?" Zack teased.

"Well, not exactly," Jesse admitted. "Gran and Gramp helped me — and Sheriff Brady," he added.

Zack jumped up. "Your grandparents called the sheriff! Is he going to arrest Arnold?"

"I don't think so," Jesse said with a frown. "We still don't have any real proof that Arnold started the fire."

"Oh, well," Zack said. "At least the fire was stopped before anyone got hurt. That's what really matters."

Jesse looked up at his friend. "I guess," he said slowly. Then he added, "But if no one stops Alan Arnold, he might try something else to get the land."

Zack squatted down and patted Pegleg. "Does the sheriff have any clues?" he asked.

"No good ones," Jesse told him. "All he knows for sure is that the fire started near the stand of royal palms."

"Where's that?"

"Back behind the office. Sheriff Brady found the cap to a gasoline can there. It was lying under a poisonwood tree." Jesse put his hand on Pegleg's head. The little dog was getting restless. "Take it easy," Jesse told him.

"I've got an idea," Zack said, his eyes shining with excitement. "Let's take

Pegleg and go have a look around."

"Where?" Jesse asked him.

Zack grinned. "I'll give you three guesses."

"Look at that!" Zack exclaimed when they reached the royal palms. "Those trees are so smooth and tall and straight — and they look like they've got skirts on top of them."

"Uh–huh," Jesse said. The trees would normally have interested him, too. But right now he was much more concerned with the ground around them.

"Zack," he said, "a van would leave tire tracks. Right?"

"Yeah," Zack said. "But the rain probably washed them away."

"I guess you're right," Jesse said. He yawned. "So what are we looking for?"

Zack shrugged. "I don't know — anything that would prove Alan Arnold set that fire, I guess." He yanked his Mets cap out of his pocket and put it on. "My detective hat," he explained with a grin.

"Now I *know* we'll find something," Jesse said.

But after half an hour of searching, Zack slumped to the ground and leaned back against a tree trunk. "It's hot," he complained. "I'm wiped out."

"Me, too," Jesse admitted, dropping down beside him. "Let's go back to your house," he said. "We're never going to find anything anyway. Come on, Pegleg," he called, giving a whistle. But Pegleg didn't come.

Jesse looked around, worried. The little dog was nowhere in sight. "Pegleg!" he called louder. But still no dog.

Jesse frowned. "I don't like this," he said. "See those muddy pools?" He pointed one out to Zack. "Gran was telling me that during the dry season, alligators go wherever there's water. Pegleg's already been in a fight with one, you know."

Zack tried to look cheerful. "Don't worry," he told Jesse. "Pegleg's got to be around here *some*where. Maybe he's looking for clues, too."

"Hey! There he is," Jesse cried as he caught a glimpse of Pegleg's tail sticking out from behind a tree trunk some fifty yards away. The little dog was sniffing at something on the ground.

"You can't keep a good nose down," Zack teased.

The two boys waited as Pegleg came loping toward them. The dog's mouth was open slightly, and there was something shiny in his teeth.

Zack burst out laughing. "You're going to need a warehouse soon to store all the junk that Pegleg brings you!"

Jesse started laughing, too. But when he saw what Pegleg had brought him this time, he began jumping up and down. "Look at that!" he cried.

"At what?"

Jesse reached down to take the object away from Pegleg. "This!" he said as he held out a shiny pen. "This is just like the one Alan Arnold has!"

"Easy, Half-pint," Zack said. "Lots of people have gold pens."

"Right," Jesse said. He turned the pen over in his hands. Suddenly he smiled.

"What?" said Zack.

"Lots of people may have gold pens . . . but not with the initials AA on them."

"Good man," Zack said. With his forefinger, he marked a point for Jesse on an imaginary scoreboard. "You are absolutely cor-*rect!*" he said in a phony foreign accent. "The pen has to belong to Alan Arnold. . . . And here it is at the scene of the crime" — Zack stroked a panting Pegleg — "discovered by the world's most famous dog detective."

As soon as Jesse got home, he showed the new clue to his grandfather.

"Aha," Gramp exclaimed when Jesse finished telling his story. "Pegleg strikes again!" He took the pen and turned it

around and around in his fingers. It gleamed in the sunlight shining through the kitchen window.

Jesse's face was shining, too.

"So," Gramp said, "Pegleg found this, eh?"

Jesse nodded. "I bet you can't guess who lost it," he said.

"Alan Arnold!" Gramp said without a moment's hesitation.

Jesse sank back into his chair. "How did you know that?"

Gramp laughed. "Well, the letters AA are a clue. But that's not what tipped me off."

Jesse felt confused. "It isn't?"

Gramp shook his head. "You see," he told Jesse, "I saw this very pen fall out of Alan Arnold's pocket while I was giving him a tour of the farm the other day." Gramp scratched his forehead. "Let's see," he said. "I remember warning Arnold when I picked it up and gave it back to him. I told him he'd better find a safer place for that pen. But he acted like he didn't hear me. He just put the pen back in the same pocket."

"Maybe it fell out again a few minutes later," Jesse said.

"Oh, no," Gramp said. "It was still there when Arnold got into his van and drove away. So you see," Gramp went on, "Arnold *didn't* lose that pen when he was with me." He sat up straighter. "And you say Pegleg found it near the place where the fire started?"

Jesse moved his head up and down very fast.

"Well, then," Gramp said, "I'd say Alan Arnold has a whole lot of explaining to do."

Jesse threw his arms around his grandfather's neck. He was helping Gran and Gramp. He was really helping them!

"What's all this about?" Gran asked, coming into the room.

Jesse was almost bursting as he told her all about Pegleg and the pen. "Isn't that great?" he said. "Now we can put Alan Arnold in jail for a trillion years!"

"A trillion?" Gran said.

Jesse grinned. "And then Alan Arnold will never be able to hurt the farm again."

Gramp pulled Jesse down on his knee and said, "Now, hold on there, Sport. Finding Arnold's pen was a good thing. But I'm not sure it's enough to put the man in jail."

Jesse's face fell.

"It's certainly a start, though," Gramp said, tousling his grandson's hair.

Gran leaned closer to Jesse. "We'll call Sheriff Brady right now," she said, "and tell him about Pegleg's discovery. Maybe he can find out a little more about the mysterious Alan Arnold."

Chapter Ten

—◆—

A Dog for Jesse

The next morning the sheriff's car pulled up in front of the Quinn house. Jesse ran to the door to let him in.

"Gramp!" he called. "Sheriff Brady is here!"

Gramp came down the stairs and shook hands with the sheriff.

"Well, Tom," the sheriff said, "you were right. I had that lawyer of yours give Arnold a call, like you suggested. He's almost sure Arnold's voice is the same as that Sam Smith who's been trying to buy your land."

"Wow!" Jesse said. "Isn't that all you need to put Arnold in jail? That and the pen Pegleg found?"

Sheriff Brady smiled. "Not necessarily, young man," he answered. "But we'll do what we can. Now let's get a move on, Tom. Mr. Arnold's expecting me."

"But I bet he's not expecting *me*," Gramp said, following the sheriff out the door.

Later, Gran went out to examine the animals on the farm to make sure none had been injured by smoke. Jesse went over to visit Zack.

Jesse found his friend in his usual place, the hammock. "Why so gloomy?" Zack asked as Jesse plopped down on a tree stump.

Jesse shrugged. "I just wish we could be sure . . ." he said.

"Sure of what?"

"That we have enough proof to put Alan Arnold in jail for a long time."

"Listen," Zack said. "No matter what, at least Arnold will be scared off. That's the important thing. Now the farm will be safe."

"I guess so," Jesse said, cheering up again. "Thanks to you — "

"And you," Zack added.

"And the great dog detective!" they both said together. Smiling, Zack bent down to tie his sneakers, and Pegleg ran up and licked his nose.

"I wish I could see Alan Arnold's face when he sees the sheriff show up with Gramp," Jesse said.

"Yeah, he won't be able to squirm out of this one," Zack laughed, but then suddenly became serious.

"What's wrong?" Jesse asked.

"I'm leaving tomorrow," Zack said.

"You are?" Jesse gulped. "When tomorrow?"

"In the morning," Zack answered. "Early."

"But Tim and Arden are coming home *tonight* — late. Now you won't be able to meet them!"

Zack managed a grin. "Then you'll be my one and only Florida friend."

Jesse swallowed again. "Why do you have to go so soon?" he said.

"My father called from New York," Zack said. "He wants me to come back a week early so we can go on a rafting trip before school starts."

Jesse hesitated before getting up from the tree stump. "I guess this is it, then," he said. "Gran wants *me* home early."

Zack pulled his baseball cap out of his back pocket and put it on Jesse's head. "Be a good half-pint," he said.

Jesse reached up and touched the cap. "I will," he said. "And by the time I see you again, I'll be a good quart."

Zack laughed.

Jesse turned away and started walking. But then he stopped and looked back at Zack. "*Will* I see you again?"

"You can bet on it," Zack said.

Jesse tried to smile, but suddenly he wanted to be far away from Zack. He wanted the good-bye to be over. There were so many things he would have liked to say, and there wasn't time for any of them.

"Let's go, Pegleg," he said. "Gran and Gramp and Ginger are waiting for us."

But Pegleg and Zack were saying their own good-byes.

"You know what?" Zack told Jesse. "I think I'm going to miss this guy almost as much as I'm going to miss you. I've never known such a great dog."

"You wouldn't say that if you'd had a chance to meet Ginger," Jesse said. "Now, there's a great dog. She's so well-behaved and — "

"I guess . . ." Zack agreed uncertainly. He hesitated, red-faced, before continuing. "This may sound stupid," he said, "but there's something about Pegleg . . . just being around him makes me feel happy. You know what I mean?"

Jesse wasn't sure he did. Still, as he watched Zack wrap his arms around the little dog, he suddenly had a terrible thought: What if Pegleg weren't in his life anymore? What if he were gone, just like Zack would be gone?

Jesse couldn't stop himself — he slapped his hands on his knees. "Pegleg!" he called. "Here, Pegleg!"

Tail wagging and tongue flapping, Pegleg whipped around and ran straight to Jesse. He looked every bit as silly as ever, but for once Jesse didn't care. In fact, he decided, Pegleg wasn't really all that weird-looking. He was just a little unusual — a one-of-a-kind dog.

Of course, there was still Ginger to think about. Jesse loved her, too. He felt proud to be seen with her. But she'd be happy in any good home — his heart told him that. Pegleg, however, was another story altogether. All-at-once-beautiful Pegleg would be happy only with *him!*

Jesse opened his arms and Pegleg jumped up and knocked him over. That was okay with Jesse. He hugged Pegleg so hard that for once the little dog couldn't even move.

That night Tim and Arden came home, brimming with news about the bird rescue. When they'd finished telling Jesse, Gran, and Gramp all about their trip, Arden turned to her grandfather and said, "Did anything exciting happen here while we were gone?"

Gramp grinned and winked at Jesse. "Nothing Jesse couldn't handle," he said.

Jesse winked back at Gramp before burying his face in Pegleg's coat.

"Nothing *we* couldn't handle," he whispered.